SCHMOE WHITE AND THE SEVEN DORFS

by Mike Thaler
Illustrated by Jared Lee

SCHOLASTIC INC.
New York Toronto London Auckland Sydney

For Dr. Z.,
who heals with wisdom and love
— M.T.

To Mike,
Partner. Friend. Stinker.
— J.L.

ISBN 0-590-89824-8

Text copyright © 1997 by Mike Thaler.
Illustrations copyright © 1997 by Jared D. Lee Studio, Inc.
All rights reserved. Published by Scholastic Inc.
HAPPILY EVER LAUGHTER is a trademark of Mike Thaler and Jared Lee.
Library of Congress Catalog Card Number: 95-73096.

12 11 10 9 8 7 6 5 4   9/9 0 1 2/0

Printed in the U.S.A.   24

First Scholastic printing, March 1997

Once upon a time, about 2:15,
there was a lovely girl named Schmoe White.
She lived with her evil, rotten stepmother,
the Wicked Queen.

The Wicked Queen was very vain.
She spent every morning putting on her face—
false eyelashes, false eyebrows,
false lips, fake nails, and a real wig.

At noon she would gaze up
at her mirror and say,
"Mirror, mirror, on the ceiling,
which lady is the most appealing?"
One day the mirror replied,
"Even though you're outta sight,
the prettiest lady is Schmoe White.
And mirrors never lie."

The Wicked Queen flew into such a rage
that her false eyelashes fell off.
She called for her huntsman, Hugh.
"Hugh, I have a job for you!"

"Okey-dokey," said the huntsman, who was paid by the hour.
"I want you to take Schmoe White into the woods
and cut out her heart," said the Wicked Queen.
"Why—was she late for school again?" asked Hugh.
"Just do it!" screamed the Wicked Queen,
poking him with a press-on fingernail.

So Hugh took Schmoe into the woods,
but he didn't have the heart to kill her.
He just took away her compass and trail mix,
and left her alone.

"I'm lost," said Schmoe.
She was about to cry
when she heard lively music.

She followed the beat until she came to a cottage.
Peeking in the window,
she saw seven little dudes playing rock and roll.
She waited for their break and went in.

"I'm Schmoe White," she said.

"Hi, I'm Nerdy," said one of the little dudes.

"Yeah, but what's your name?" asked Schmoe.

"I'm Nerdy."

"I can see that," said Schmoe, "but what's your name?"

Nerdy rolled his eyes and pointed to the others.
"This is Grouchy on bass,
Funky on vibes,
Smiley on washboard,
Wheezy on kazoo,
Drowsy on cymbals,
and Hip on drums.
We're The Seven Dorfs.
Perhaps you've heard of us?"
"No," said Schmoe. "Do you need a lead singer?"

"Hey! That's what we're missing!" said Nerdy,
who was the brains of the outfit.
"We'll call ourselves 'Schmoe White and the Seven Dorfs,' "
said Schmoe.
"Why do you get top billing?" asked Grouchy.
"Because if it weren't for me, you wouldn't be in this story,"
replied Schmoe.

So the group began to play small gigs around the forest.
They played The Bunny Hop, The Owl Hoot,
The Turkey Trot, and The Beaver Ball.

Meanwhile, back at the castle, the Wicked Queen was gluing on her seven-foot eyelashes.

When she finished, she looked down at her mirror.
"Mirror, mirror, on the floor,
what girl's got a whole lot more?"
The mirror replied, "Well, old Queen, you're outta sight,
but the prettiest is still Schmoe White."

The Wicked Queen flew into a rage,
called Hugh, her huntsman,
and took away all his merit badges.

"If you want things done right,
you have to do them yourself,"
snarled the Queen.
So she brewed up a batch of her deadliest poison,
dipped a lipstick into it,
combed her wig over her face,
and hurried off to the Dorfs' cottage.
She rapped on the door.

"Who's there?" asked Schmoe.

"The Rave-On Lady," answered the Queen.

"I don't wear makeup," said Schmoe, opening the door.

"But we're having a special on lipstick," insisted the Queen.

"It's called Pass-Out Pink. Try a free sample!"

"Well, okay," said Schmoe,
who didn't want to hurt the Rave-On Lady's feelings.
She put on some lipstick.

"Enjoy!" cackled the Queen,
and she ran off into the forest.
Schmoe waved good-bye. Then she fell down.

"Schmoe's fainted!" said Nerdy, when the Dorfs came home.

"She's resting," said Drowsy.

"She's cleaning the floor," said Funky.

"She's looking for her contact lens," said Smiley.

"She must have allergies," said Wheezy.

"She's blocking the doorway," said Grouchy.

"She's dead," said Hip.

The Seven Dorfs began to cry into their beards.

Just then, a handsome prince knocked on the door.

"Hi, we just lost our lead vocalist," said Nerdy.

"I sing a little," said the prince.

"What's your name?" asked the Dorfs, wringing out their beards.

"Prince," said the prince. "We could be 'Prince and the Seven Dorfs.' "

"What should we do with Schmoe White?" asked Nerdy.

"I'll kiss her and she'll probably wake up," said the prince.

He did. And she woke up!
And then the prince died.

"Who's he, and why is he wearing pink lipstick?" asked Schmoe.
"He's a prince, and I think he's wearing Drop-Dead Red," said Smiley.
"Well," said Schmoe, "I'll kiss him and he'll probably wake up."

She did. And he woke up!

And then Schmoe died again.

So the prince kissed her, and she woke up, and he died again.

This went on so long that they gave up their singing careers.

The Seven Dorfs broke up
and started a baseball team with seven shortstops.

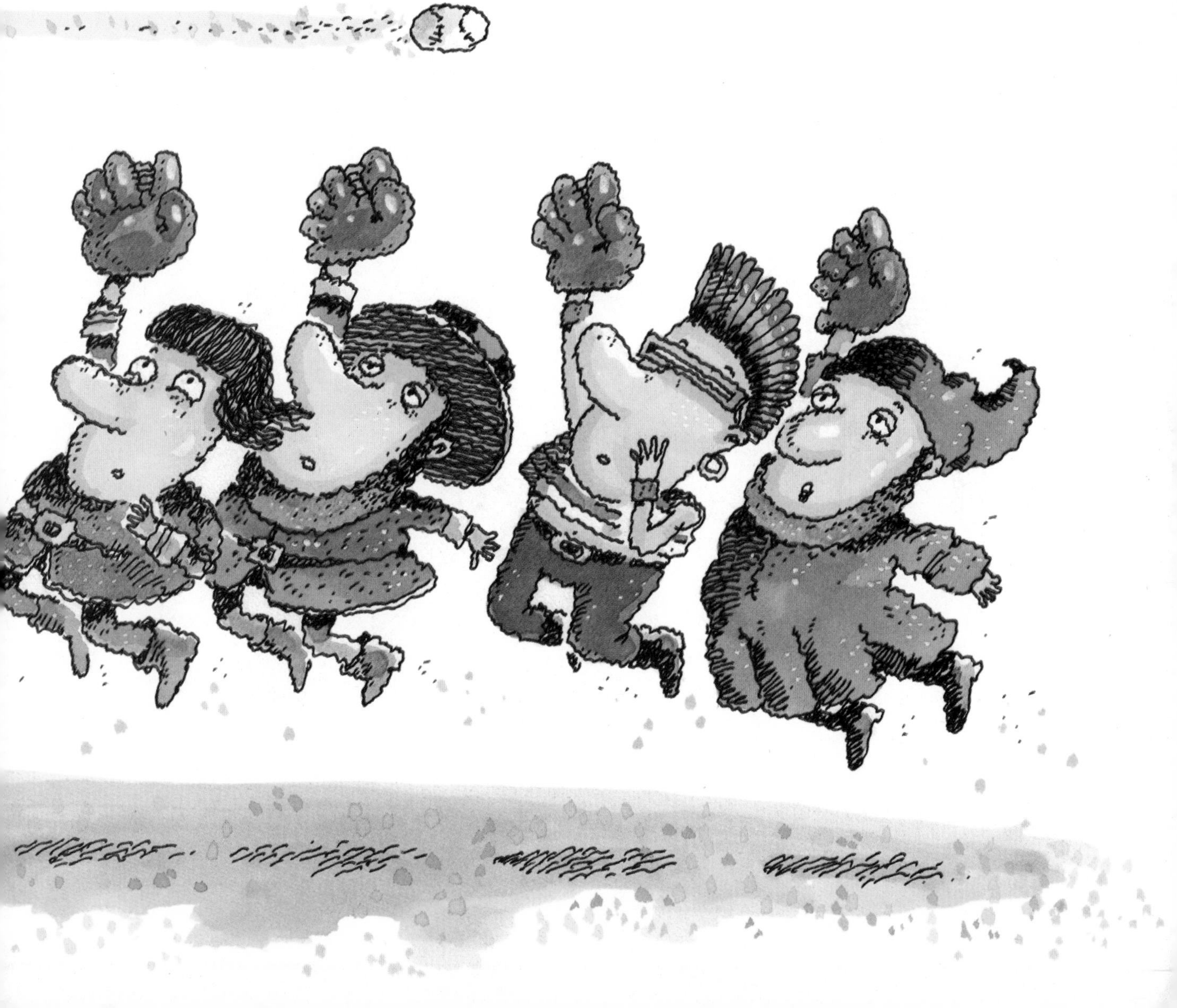

By the way, the Wicked Queen
entered the Miss New Jersey Contest and placed second.
Her mirror placed first.

THE END